A MESSAGE TO PARENTS

Reading good books to young children is a crucial factor in a child's psychological and intellectual development. It promotes a mutually warm and satisfying relationship between parent and child and enhances the child's awareness of the world around him. It stimulates the child's imagination and lays a foundation for the development of the skills necessary to support the critical thinking process. In addition, the parent who reads to his child helps him to build vocabulary and other prerequisite skills for the child's own successful reading.

In order to provide parents and children with books which will do these things, Brown Watson has published this series of small books specially designed for young children. These books are factual, fanciful, humorous, questioning and adventurous. A library acquired in this inexpensive way will provide many hours of pleasurable and profitable reading for parents and children.

Aladdin

Text by Maureen Spurgeon

Brown Watson
ENGLAND

Art and text copyright © 1990 Brown Watson Ltd. England.
All rights reserved.
Printed and bound in Germany
STARTRIGHT ELF and the Startright Elf logo are trademarks of
Checkerboard Press, Inc. USA. 0 9 8 7 6 5 4 3 2 1

ONCE upon a time, in one of the very oldest cities in ancient China, there lived a poor widow, and her son, who was called Aladdin.

Aladdin was a good boy, always bright and cheerful and ready to help people whenever he could.

And to help his mother, he would go to the market once or twice a week.

One day in the market place, a man said he had a job for Aladdin. "You will be well paid," he said.

The man led Aladdin to a secret cave. "I want you to climb down this rope," he said. "I am too fat to get through the hole myself, you see."

When his feet touched the floor of the cave, he could hardly believe what he saw! Chests and boxes, all filled with treasure!

"Stop dreaming!" shouted the man, his voice hard and cruel. "Start tying everything to the rope, so that I can pull it up here!"

It was hard work, tying on all the treasures. But Aladdin kept thinking of the money he had been promised, and all he could buy for his mother!

"My turn, now!" cried Aladdin, when he had finished.

The man tugged the rope away.

"Set you free to let everyone know my secret?"

And with an evil laugh, the man thundered away, leaving Aladdin trapped in the underground cave with no food, no water, no money . . . nothing, except one thing . . .

The lamp did not look very special. But Aladdin began rubbing it. At once, there was a whooshing sound, and a bright flash of light!

"I am the genie of the lamp!"
said a deep voice, the huge eyes
of the genie twinkling at the look
of amazement on Aladdin's face.
"Your wish is my command!"

"I'd like something to take to my mother!" Aladdin burst out. Next minute, he was in another treasure cave, even bigger than the first!

"Take whatever you wish," smiled the genie. "Then my magic carpet will take you home. Just rub the lamp whenever you need me, and I will come at once."

Aladdin's mother could hardly believe what she saw!

"No more worries about having enough money for food!" he told her proudly. "We're rich, now!"

Before long, Aladdin and his mother had the most wonderful mansion which the genie built by magic! Even the Emperor was impressed by what he saw!

Such a handsome, wealthy young man would be the ideal husband for his daughter, he thought. And how proud Aladdin's mother was to see her son marry a beautiful princess!

By this time, the man who had left Aladdin in the underground cave was so jealous! How, he wondered, had Aladdin got his riches? He decided to watch him, every hour of the day.

At last, his patience was rewarded. As soon as he saw Aladdin rubbing his magic lamp and the genie appearing, he guessed what the secret was! The magic lamp should be his, he decided!

He put on the clothes of a pedlar, and went to the street where Aladdin lived.

"New lamps for old!" he cried, ringing a bell. "New lamps for old!"

It sounded a bargain to the emperor's daughter. But Aladdin was very angry, and guessed who had taken the lamp.

Sure enough, at the market next day — the man was there, selling the treasures the genie had got for him. Aladdin knew he would not risk bringing the magic lamp to the market . . .

So, he followed him home, waiting for his chance to snatch the magic lamp, give it a rub and make the genie appear!

"Take this man away to a far-off land!" he commanded.

"Very good, Master!" roared the genie. "Your wish is my command!"

The man tried to escape, but the magic power of the genie was stronger than any man!

How he wished then that he had not been so greedy!

As for Aladdin, he was overjoyed to see the genie again, welcoming him home like the true friend he was!

From now on, he said, the genie should live like a real person.